the BugaBees

friends with food allergies

by Amy Recob

Illustrated by 64 Colors

BEAVER'S POND
PRESS

ISBN 13: 978-1-59298-279-0

Library of Congress Catalog Number: 2009924662
Printed in the United States of America
Third Printing: 2012
14 13   12   5 4 3

Cover and interior design by 64 Colors

Beaver's Pond Press, Inc.
7108 Ohms Lane,
Edina, MN 55439-2129
(952) 829-8818
www.BeaversPondPress.com

To order, visit www.BeaverspondBooks.com or call (800) 901-3480.
Reseller discounts available.

For Mollie Rose,
The most precious BugaBee of all

A portion of the proceeds from this book will help fund programs dedicated to food allergy research, treatment, and prevention.

For more information, visit www.thebugabees.com.

Some of the scenarios portrayed in this book are applicable
to more than one food allergy, and not all food allergies are alike.
Reactions and their level of severity can vary greatly depending on the
individual and the level of food allergen exposure. Always consult your doctor
for the most appropriate treatment and course of action for your situation.

Introducing...

the
BugaBees

This is the story of eight BugaBees–
A great bunch of friends with food allergies.
They always have fun and they never feel blue
Unless they eat foods they're allergic to.

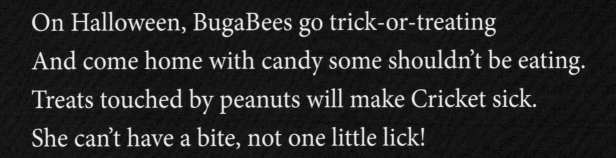

On Halloween, BugaBees go trick-or-treating
And come home with candy some shouldn't be eating.
Treats touched by peanuts will make Cricket sick.
She can't have a bite, not one little lick!

"No thank you," she says. "It's really okay.
I can still have lots of fun without peanuts anyway."

Later, they celebrate Firefly's birthday.
But no milkshakes for Beetle; there just is no way.
Foods made with milk Beetle really can't eat.
He could be covered in hives from his head to his feet!

"No thank you," he says. "It's really okay.
I can still have lots of fun without milk anyway."

At school, the lunch special is fish sticks with fries.
"I'm allergic to fish!" little Ladybug cries.
"I need something different for lunch if you please,
Like spaghetti or pizza or perhaps a grilled cheese?"

"Oh thank you," she says. "It's really okay.
I can still have lots of fun without fish anyway."

At a fun weekend picnic, Caterpillar is sad.
All the foods made with wheat will make him feel bad.
"Don't worry," says Mommy.
"You can have other good things.
Now let's play in the park on the
slide and the swings."

"Oh thank you," he says. "It's really okay.
I can still have lots of fun without wheat anyway."

In summer, if seafood is served at the beach,
All shrimp, crab, and shellfish are kept out of reach.
Butterfly could just taste one and start to feel ill
And need to be treated with a shot or a pill.

"No thank you," she says. "It's really okay.
I can still have lots of fun without shellfish anyway."

When dining at breakfast, if Bumblebee eats eggs,
He could start to feel swelling in his face, hands, and legs.
Of course, he knows better and stays far away
From foods made with eggs so he can focus on play.

"No thank you," he says. "It's really okay.
I can still have lots of fun without eggs anyway."

During free time, sweet Firefly always takes care
Not to eat tree nuts in the treats her friends share.
If she ever ate walnuts, pecans, or cashews,
All the food in her stomach she could suddenly lose!

LIBRARY

"No thank you," she says. "It's really okay.
I can still have lots of fun without tree nuts anyway."

Cookies and crackers and foods made with soy,
Could make our dear Dragonfly one very sick boy.
So he always checks labels on foods that he eats,
And fresh fruits and veggies are his favorite safe treats!

"No thank you," he says. "It's really okay.
I can still have lots of fun without soy anyway."

So whether it's peanuts or tree nuts or fish,
Or some other ingredient put in a dish,
That makes you feel queasy or itchy or yucky,
It means you're allergic, but also quite lucky
To have such good friends, and a great family,
Who love you so dearly, like a sweet BugaBee!

BugaBees Activities & Talking Points

The best way to protect a child from a serious allergic reaction is through awareness and prevention. The following pages are provided to help adults engage children in early discussions about how to stay healthy and happy in spite of a food allergy diagnosis.

Knowing what symptoms to watch for, which foods to avoid, and what questions to ask are all key factors in successfully managing a food allergy. Remembering that there is much fun to be had – despite the need to say "no thank you" to certain foods – is also essential in helping develop strong emotional health and well-being.

While BugaBee characters are intended to provide a general guideline for managing children's food allergies, it is important to acknowledge that not all food allergies are alike. Reactions and their level of severity can vary greatly depending on the individual and the level of food allergen exposure. Always consult your doctor for the most appropriate treatment and course of action for your situation.

Cricket is allergic to peanuts

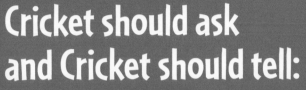

Cricket should ask and Cricket should tell:

"What's in my food? Is it safe for me?
I have a food allergy, and I want to stay well!"

1. Point to all the foods that could be dangerous for Cricket to eat.

2. What could happen if Cricket accidentally ate a dangerous food?

3. Point to all the foods that are most likely safe for Cricket to eat.

4. What is the best way for Cricket to make sure she doesn't eat foods that might have peanuts in them?

5. Missing out on certain foods doesn't mean missing out on all the fun. Some of Cricket's favorite things to do include dressing up in costumes and acting silly with friends. What are some of your favorite fun things to do?

peanuts

grapes

spaghetti

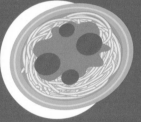

popcorn

peanut butter sandwich

SUGGESTED ANSWERS:

1. Peanuts, popcorn if made with peanut oil, peanut butter sandwich, and any other item that may have been touched by or processed in a plant that also processes peanuts. 2. All allergic reactions are different. Some give you itchy red hives on your skin. Some make it very hard to breathe. Some make you throw up. Some make you sick enough to need a shot and an emergency trip to the hospital, which is why it's so important to be careful. 3. If none of the following items have been touched by or processed in a plant that also processes peanuts: grapes, spaghetti, and popcorn if made with vegetable oil. 4. Cricket should always ask a grown-up if the food is safe to eat for someone with a peanut allergy. 5. All answers are correct!

Beetle is allergic to milk

Beetle should ask and Beetle should tell:

"What's in my food? Is it safe for me?
I have a food allergy, and I want to stay well!"

milk

strawberries

pizza

carrots

yogurt

1. Point to all the foods that could be dangerous for Beetle to eat.

2. What could happen if Beetle accidentally ate a dangerous food?

3. Point to all the foods that are most likely safe for Beetle to eat.

4. What is the best way for Beetle to make sure he doesn't eat foods that might have milk in them?

5. Missing out on certain foods doesn't mean missing out on all the fun. Some of Beetle's favorite things to do include shopping for presents and going to birthday parties. What are some of your favorite fun things to do?

Ladybug is allergic to fish

Ladybug should ask and Ladybug should tell:

"What's in my food? Is it safe for me?
I have a food allergy, and I want to stay well!"

1. Point to all the foods that could be dangerous for Ladybug to eat.

2. What could happen if Ladybug accidentally ate a dangerous food?

3. Point to all the foods that are most likely safe for Ladybug to eat.

4. What is the best way for Ladybug to make sure she doesn't eat foods that might have fish in them?

5. Missing out on certain foods doesn't mean missing out on all the fun. Some of Ladybug's favorite things to do include going to school and reading new books. What are some of your favorite fun things to do?

SUGGESTED ANSWERS:
1. Fish sticks, french fries if cooked in the same oil as fish sticks, and any other item that may have been touched by fish. 2. All allergic reactions are different. Some give you itchy red hives on your skin. Some make it very hard to breathe. Some make you throw up. Some make you sick enough to need a shot and an emergency trip to the hospital, which is why it's so important to be careful. 3. If none of the following items have been touched by fish: apple, muffin, corn, french fries if not cooked in the same oil as fish sticks. 4. Ladybug should always ask a grown-up if the food is safe to eat for someone with a fish allergy. 5. All answers are correct!

fish sticks

apple

muffin

corn

french fries

Caterpillar is allergic to wheat

Caterpillar should ask and Caterpillar should tell:

"What's in my food? Is it safe for me?
I have a food allergy, and I want to stay well!"

watermelon

bread

1. Point to all the foods that could be dangerous for Caterpillar to eat.

2. What could happen if Caterpillar accidentally ate a dangerous food?

3. Point to all the foods that are most likely safe for Caterpillar to eat.

cheese

4. What is the best way for Caterpillar to make sure he doesn't eat foods that might have wheat in them?

5. Missing out on certain foods doesn't mean missing out on all the fun. Some of Caterpillar's favorite things to do include playing outside and visiting the park with friends. What are some of your favorite fun things to do?

blueberries

SUGGESTED ANSWERS:

1. Bread if made with wheat flour, ravioli if made with wheat pasta, and any other item that may have been touched by wheat. 2. All allergic reactions are different. Some give you itchy red hives on your skin. Some make it very hard to breathe. Some make you throw up. Some make you sick enough to need a shot and an emergency trip to the hospital, which is why it's so important to be careful. 3. If none of the following items have been touched by wheat: watermelon, cheese, blueberries, bread if made with rice flour, ravioli if made with rice pasta. 4. Caterpillar should always ask a grown-up if the food is safe to eat for someone with a wheat allergy. 5. All answers are correct!

ravioli

Butterfly is allergic to shellfish

Butterfly should ask and Butterfly should tell:

"What's in my food? Is it safe for me? I have a food allergy, and I want to stay well!"

1. Point to all the foods that could be dangerous for Butterfly to eat.

2. What could happen if Butterfly accidentally ate a dangerous food?

3. Point to all the foods that are most likely safe for Butterfly to eat.

4. What is the best way for Butterfly to make sure she doesn't eat foods that might have shellfish in them?

5. Missing out on certain foods doesn't mean missing out on all the fun. Some of Butterfly's favorite things to do include going to the beach and building sand castles. What are some of your favorite fun things to do?

shrimp

pancakes

banana

orange juice

chicken nuggets

SUGGESTED ANSWERS:
1. Shrimp, chicken nuggets if cooked in the same pan as shellfish, and any other item that may have been touched by shellfish. 2. All allergic reactions are different. Some give you itchy red hives on your skin. Some make it very hard to breathe. Some make you throw up. Some make you sick enough to need a shot and an emergency trip to the hospital, which is why it's so important to be careful. 3. If none of the following items have been touched by shellfish: pancakes, banana, orange juice, chicken nuggets if not cooked in same pan as shellfish. 4. Butterfly should always ask a grown-up if the food is safe to eat for someone with a shellfish allergy. 5. All answers are correct!

Firefly is allergic to tree nuts

Firefly should ask and Firefly should tell:

"What's in my food? Is it safe for me?
I have a food allergy, and I want to stay well!"

1. Point to all the foods that could be dangerous for Firefly to eat.

2. What could happen if Firefly accidentally ate a dangerous food?

3. Point to all the foods that are most likely safe for Firefly to eat.

4. What is the best way for Firefly to make sure she doesn't eat foods that might have tree nuts in them?

5. Missing out on certain foods doesn't mean missing out on all the fun. Some of Firefly's favorite things to do include going to the library and spending time with friends. What are some of your favorite fun things to do?

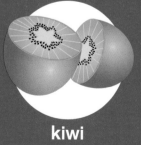

ice cream

pear

mac & cheese

sugar cookie

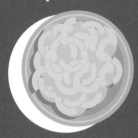

kiwi

SUGGESTED ANSWERS:
1. Ice cream and cookie if either contain nuts or are processed in a plant that also processes tree nuts, and any other item that may have been touched by tree nuts such as pecans, almonds, walnuts, and cashews. 2. All allergic reactions are different. Some give you itchy red hives on your skin. Some make it very hard to breathe. Some make you throw up. Some make you sick enough to need a shot and an emergency trip to the hospital, which is why it's so important to be careful. 3. If none of the following items have been touched by or processed in a plant that also processes tree nuts: ice cream, cookie, pear, mac and cheese, kiwi. 4. Firefly should always ask a grown-up if the food is safe to eat for someone with a tree nut allergy. 5. All answers are correct!

Bumblebee is allergic to eggs

Bumblebee should ask and Bumblebee should tell:

*"What's in my food? Is it safe for me?
I have a food allergy, and I want to stay well!"*

1. Point to all the foods that could be dangerous for Bumblebee to eat.

2. What could happen if Bumblebee accidentally ate a dangerous food?

3. Point to all the foods that are most likely safe for Bumblebee to eat.

4. What is the best way for Bumblebee to make sure he doesn't eat foods that might have eggs in them?

5. Missing out on certain foods doesn't mean missing out on all the fun. Some of Bumblebee's favorite things to do include hanging out at home and playing with his favorite toys. What are some of your favorite fun things to do?

cherries

scrambled eggs

snap peas

cake

apple juice

SUGGESTED ANSWERS:
1. Scrambled eggs, cake if made with eggs, and any other item that may have been touched by eggs. 2. All allergic reactions are different. Some give you itchy red hives on your skin. Some make it very hard to breathe. Some make you throw up. Some make you sick enough to need a shot and an emergency trip to the hospital, which is why it's so important to be careful. 3. If none of the following items have been touched by or made with eggs: cherries, snap peas, cake, apple juice. 4. Bumblebee should always ask a grown-up if the food is safe to eat for someone with an egg allergy. 5. All answers are correct!

Dragonfly is allergic to soy

Dragonfly should ask and Dragonfly should tell:

"What's in my food? Is it safe for me? I have a food allergy, and I want to stay well!"

1. Point to all the foods that could be dangerous for Dragonfly to eat.
2. What could happen if Dragonfly accidentally ate a dangerous food?
3. Point to all the foods that are most likely safe for Dragonfly to eat.
4. What is the best way for Dragonfly to make sure he doesn't eat foods that might have soy in them?
5. Missing out on certain foods doesn't mean missing out on all the fun. Some of Dragonfly's favorite things to do include eating fresh fruits and vegetables and picking apples at the orchard near his house. What are some of your favorite fun things to do?

bagel

raisins

pineapple

tomato soup

crackers

SUGGESTED ANSWERS:
1. Crackers if made with soy, and any other item that may contain or have been touched by soy.
2. All allergic reactions are different. Some give you itchy red hives on your skin. Some make it very hard to breathe. Some make you throw up. Some make you sick enough to need a shot and an emergency trip to the hospital, which is why it's so important to be careful. 3. If none of the following items have been touched by or made with soy: bagel, tomato soup, crackers, raisins, pineapple. 4. Dragonfly should always ask a grown-up if the food is safe to eat for someone with a soy allergy. 5. All answers are correct!